when the world didn't end

poems

when the world didn't end

poems

Caroline Kaufman

illustrations by Yelena Bryksenkova

HARPER

An Imprint of HarperCollinsPublishers

ISBN 978-0-06-291038-7

Typography by Jenna Stempel-Lobell
19 20 21 22 23   PC/LSCH   10 9 8 7 6 5 4 3 2 1
❖
First Edition

*to the little girl who never cared
what anyone else thought.*

*I've missed you.
welcome home.*

Contents

a lot of my life has focused on surviving. I told myself I needed to push through my worst days so that I could make it out alive. and I did. but that was when I realized I wanted more out of life than just survival. I wanted to laugh and love and breathe and kiss and sing. I wanted to *live*. and for me, that required facing a lot of trauma. it required facing a lot of difficult experiences, particularly in relation to mental illness, suicidal ideation, self-harm, disordered eating, and sexual assault. so if it's too hard for you to read about these topics, I get it. please take care of yourself, reach out for help, and do whatever you need to do to stay safe. these are not easy things to talk about, hear about, or read about. but I include all of it. because sometimes talking and hearing and reading can help you heal. I include all of it because writing about the past is what finally allowed me to move forward.

go write the poem.

"what poem?"

the poem you're incapable of writing.

what was

we prepared for the worst.
for disaster.
stockpiling canned soup and batteries
and gallons of water and first-aid kits
as if there was some chance at survival.

we marked our calendars.
counted down the days.
and no one would admit it,
but we were calm.
nothing prepared us for the calm.
for the comfort.
for the relief that we would never
have to clean up the mess we created.

but then,
we opened up a window and saw

that the world was still there.
and to be honest,
none of us knew what to do.

survival was the only outcome
we weren't prepared for.

arithmetic

I still count on my fingers.
you laugh as I lay my hands out
on the table like a small child,
trying to add the tip to the total.

you tell me you
have never seen someone
fly through calculus
but still get stuck on
elementary school mathematics.

but that's how it's always been—
the complicated easy.
the simple more difficult.
and it's okay, for a while,
until you wake up and you're
an adult and you don't know

how to take care of yourself.
until you wake up and you're
an adult and you don't know
how to ask for help.

I was so distracted by
getting to the finish line
that I forgot to pace myself.

I was so distracted by growing up
that I forgot the basics along the way.

sometimes I try to keep
my pain close to the surface.
because I am scared that people
will no longer want me
once my memory
of the hurt runs out.
once there is no more sadness
to fill these pages.

it is so easy to
reopen closed wounds
when people see my bloodshed
as beautiful.

the only thing I know about
what sits underneath my skin
is that it is full of
lack of matter.
and I am trying to regurgitate
the nothingness but it is
getting caught in my throat.

maybe nothing was poetic
the first few times
but it has now lost its meaning
and turned back into nothing.

maybe I was poetic
the first few times
I dug out all of this hollow
but my emptiness does not
resemble a poem anymore.

maybe it never did
in the first place.

I am a book
with the pages all worn.

the cover is tearing,
the ink is fading,

but I swear I'm worth the read.

little girl wears pigtails. little girl is not afraid of anything, even monsters in the closet. little girl splatter-paints the walls and is proud of it. little girl puts her hair in a ponytail and then chops it all off. little girl does not have much hair for a while. little girl is brave. little girl is kind. little girl cries when she holds a hamster for the first time. little girl teaches herself how to roll her *r*'s and make a taco tongue all by herself. little girl loves to dance and sing and run around during recess. little girl wears big pink goggles when she goes swimming. little girl is strong. little girl is determined.

tomorrow morning I will promise
to see this nothing as everything.

and tomorrow night I will forgive myself
for not being able to.

and the next morning I will promise again.
and the next night I will forgive again.

and none of it will mean anything at all.

picardy third

you're getting good at tying things up
in a neat little bow,
at molding wrapping paper
around your misshapen ideas.
you'll tape it all together.
maybe stick a ribbon on top.
hope no one will notice the pain and the hurt
if it all comes in a presentable little package.

you're getting good at remembering
to say *just kidding*
at the end of every self-deprecating joke.
at tagging on an *lol* when
the text seems too angry.
queen of backtracking,
champion of invalidating your own feelings,
a professional at wanting them to understand,
but also wanting them to stay comfortable.

you're getting good at ending
on a positive note.
on a high note,
just a half step above what they're all
expecting.

because maybe if you write
an entire poem on self-loathing,
just to say something nice
in the very last line,
that will balance out everything else.

(we both know that will not
balance out everything else.)
but sometimes it's nice to pretend.
to hope a bit of good will outweigh the bad.

to believe changing one note in the final chord
will make them forget
they were ever in a minor key at all.

I cannot turn this
art project of a person
into heart and soul.

all I know to do
is cover my skin in clay
and beg you to sculpt.

make me beautiful,
I whisper. *I only want*
to be who you want.

*messages he sent me, or a list of reasons why I still
hold a grudge:*

*so do you spit or swallow? / there is a wrong and
a right answer / stop worrying so much / you
have no self-esteem / gotta step up your game / I
am a teenage boy / guys are weird / it's not hard
/ **relationships are about compromises right**
/ you just worry about everything so much / not
saying its entirely your fault / maybe you're just
not that into me / literally nothing to be afraid of
/ I'm not that mean / I'm not scary / **its not like
you wont have fun** / I'm sure once you get a taste
you won't be able to get enough / I mean gotta do
it eventually / I wouldn't hesitate / whoops sorry /
so sorry / **I mean you know how guys are** / did
you mind? / you dodged the question / I should stop
doing that / I really don't want to hurt you / oh shit
did I trap you? / I must have been real hormoned*

up and quite dumb / **so you do really hate it that much** / hope I can change that somehow / it would be real nice if you wanted it / took me two months to get you alone / **I like to think you enjoy it a little** / you got ur hormone levels or whatever checked right? / I want you to like it / I still want to see if you will / I'm sure its worth a shot / is your name homework? cause I'm not doing you / **but I should be** / so guess that's a no / well fak now I just wanna try more / I have some nice friends / I don't tell them / **but if I did they would say dump your ungrateful ass** / iunno guess its selfish of me / I'm a bad person / sometimes I really wish you felt stuff / youre not into it / feel free to prove me wrong / you thought you would hate it but you tried it / there is somehow hope for you / **why can't we be normal** / you're making it hard / you crazy man / you always worry for no reason / don't worry / you already know what I wanna do / u can fix that / **I just wanna get you comfortable** / I want u to wanna / you don't trust me at all / you didn't wanna do anything and you made it this far / I wanna make it fun for you / **yeah I'll have to step up my game then** / I'll surprise you instead / sounds like fun no? / I'm bad at knowing when

*I'm pushing / I should stop doing that / dont let me try to pull anything tomorrow ok? / will be better tmrw / well shit / youre torture / **still think you would enjoy it** / I would do anything / so guess that's a no / yeah I blame you / **sorry in advance** / like you too much / whoops sorry / that was fun / hope you had fun / well fak / yeah sorry / **that bad huh?** / well who do I bang now / I was hoping that would be you / **u sure the anti-paranoia meds are working?** / pull yourself together / you always are paranoid and dramatic / you worry too much / **my god you're crazy** / we're done thanks / there was no way we could work if you had no trust in me / coulda had some fun / what a shame*

I'm sorry if you are bored
of always seeing my pain overflow.

but if I do not let it
pool between my hands,
I will have nothing else to give you.

as a kid,
I could never decide
on my favorite season.

I would watch the first leaves
start to turn golden
on the edges,
and swear that fall was my favorite.

and then,
late november would
bring the first snowfall
with a few flurries in the night,
and I would smile and promise
that it was winter.

the buds on the trees
would start to peek out,

and suddenly
my favorite was spring.
school would end, and I'd
change my mind—
it was definitely summer.

and looking back,
it's such a beautiful idea:
to have your favorite moment
be the moment right in front of you.
looking back,
that's all I ever wanted.

for the best part of my life
to always be the present.

how it all ends
after t. s. eliot

this is the way the world ends
a fade off into the night
not with a bang but a whimper
a muted dying of the light

this is the way our lives end
our pulses will fade away
no final words in the heat of the moment
rather, dusk at the end of our day

this is the way that we end
the anticlimactic goodbye
not with a flame but a whisper
no strength left in us to try

I go to the doctor
with one request:
cut it out of my brain.
make me forget it ever happened.

they tell me that's not possible,
they're sorry,
they cannot help me.

how am I supposed to
move on then?

every night, when I walk home,
I check to see if my shoulders
are any smoother.

I'm always hoping your touch
is soft enough to
wear away at my rough edges.

I have made a career out of never letting go.
I keep a closed fist on every bad memory
and refuse to loosen my grip.
most people can learn to release.
they learn that the past must slip
through your fingers in order for
your hands to become clean again.
in order to start over.

but I don't want to start over.
this is all I know how to do.
I do not love my trauma.
but at least it is something to
wrap my hands around.
at least it is something
to keep me busy.

at least it will be considered art
to the people around me.

I'm not saying I wanted to die,
but I was ready for it.

in that moment,
the only thing I feared more
than having to die
was having to survive.

the only thing I feared more
than having to break
was having to rebuild.

little girl becomes girl. girl reads above grade
level and knows her times tables before anyone
else in her class. girl breaks a lot of bones
but doesn't really care. girl is smart. girl is
passionate. girl learns how to snowboard and
play guitar. girl finally understands the word
lonely. girl tries keeping a diary but feels like
the words never come out right. girl figures
out how to use the scale in her room. girl uses
the scale in her room. girl likes a girl for the
first time. girl is confused. girl is talented. girl
sings the solo in her chorus concert and gets
complimented on it for the next few weeks.
girl grows out of her jeans and feels bad about
it, but doesn't understand why. girl is stressed.
girl is trying.

it's funny how you wrap up the hurt
like a birthday present
before you hand it to me.

you dig into my body—
blood and guts everywhere—
and then tie my intestines
into a neat little bow
on top of it all.

you say *look at how
beautiful you are now, baby.
it's a gift from me to you.*

and I say *thank you.*
and I say *thank you.*
and all I know to say
is *thank you.*

most days,
my depression
is just a piece of me.

other days,
I am just a piece
of my depression.

—*it is one of those days.*

every time I speak,
I fear my voice is too loud.
I listen to the walls for an echo
every time I take a breath.

something in me feels like
I am not allotted this much existence—
I am taking up space
that does not belong to me.

this universe is infinite,
and still,

I occupy too much of it.

when I was twelve,
all the sharp objects
were taken out of my room.

no shaving razors,
no scissors,
no thumbtacks,
no staples.

anything I could possibly
hurt myself with
was held under lock and key.

for all of high school,
I could not cut out drawings
or use a stapler
without my mind wandering.

we dissected frogs freshman year
and all I could think about
was splaying myself open.

it's strange now
to tack pictures up on my wall
and not think anything of it.
to pry a staple out
and instinctively pull back my hand
when I feel the sharp edge
poking into my skin.

it's strange,
but it's freeing.
thumbtacks are just thumbtacks.
staples are just staples.
and nothing else ever crosses my mind.

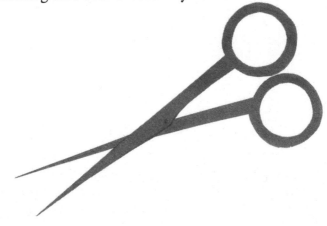

I am always so pulled in
by your presence.

gravity is your greatest strength
and my greatest weakness.

there are days
I do not recognize
myself in the mirror.

my reflection is
a drawing that didn't
quite get me right.

I know it's
supposed to be me,
but the face
is unfamiliar.

I just don't recognize
myself anymore.

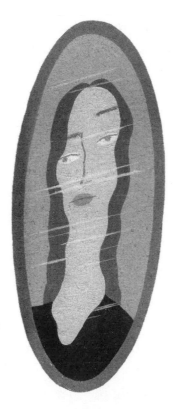

after him,
I am so scared of being hurt again.

you kiss me
again and again and again
and I still find myself whispering,
this is mutual, right?
you're sure you like me, right?
I'm not just making things up, right?

it may sound silly,
but he taught me that
someone could
love and laugh and promise
and still not be so sure.

he taught me that
someone could
love and laugh and promise
and then one day change their mind.

I know it's not healthy,
but my eyes always come back to you.
I have spent so many years
looking through telescopes,
admiring from afar.

but now you sit right in front of me,
in perfect detail.

don't tell me to look away.
you know you'd keep your eyes open, too.

I don't think
I will ever be satisfied with
all that I've done.

I do not see this life
as something you can complete.
I do not see this journey
as one that has an ending.

it is hard to be proud
of how far you've come
when there will always be
miles and miles ahead of you.

you tell me you like to run.
you talk about sneakers
and waking up early
and all the miles you have traversed.

you tell me you like to run,
and all I hear is *I will not stay.*
all I hear is *I will get scared*
and leave you behind.

all I hear is
I am so good at abandonment
that it has become a pastime.

the first time I hold a human heart in my
hands, I am in high school, wearing the nitrile
gloves, the goggles, the lab coat, I am a student
who does not want to make a mess, does not
want to get my hands dirty, does not want to
get too attached, so I put a sheet over his face,
close his eyes, I am trying not to look but
doing it anyway,

and I think about how he ended up here, how
his veins got so calcified, how they pushed all
of his ribs aside in order to get a closer look,
and how he let them, they are passing around
his heart now, one pair of purple hands to the
next, not a second thought about it, cupping
it, marveling at it, feeling its weight, pressing
fingertip and nail into muscle, holding it up
to the eye, looking through the chambers like
a telescope, a spyglass, a microscope, before
we put it gently back into his chest, where it
belongs, lock it back in with every repositioned
rib, try to make it seem like we were never
digging around there in the first place, of
course we weren't,

and so we move on to the next body, this one
open to the stomach, we put on a new pair of
gloves, and start unraveling her intestines,
I know it is a her, there is a name tag this time,
a body tag, it says how old she was, the cause
of death, and her first name, but not her last
name, in order to humanize her, but still keep
us removed, as removed as you can get when
you're wrist-deep into her abdomen, and my
fingers are traveling along her liver now, and
it is dark, and there's a lot of scarring, and
the professors says she might have been an
alcoholic, and I can see the gray hair peeking
out from under the white sheet, which makes
me think maybe she was a mom, maybe she was
a grandmother, but the bell rings before I have
time to write an obituary from her body parts,

and so we all take off our gloves and wash our
hands, and wash again, and wash again, and
try to forget about it all, but I can't forget,
because I can still feel his heart weighing down
my hands, and I can still see the liver cirrhosis
behind my eyelids, and I'm in awe of how a
pile of lifeless bones and skin can make me feel
so much, how a body can still throw punches
from the grave, how we can write a story out
of scar tissue, and it makes me want to do the
same,

to donate my body to science, to have everyone
gather around me, chest splayed open, picking
me apart, bright lights on to get a better look,
strangers pressing fingernails into my scar
tissue over and over to get a sense of what my
life was like, to make them feel what my life
was like, to not have to do all of the digging
myself, to sit back and let everyone else search
for the answers inside me for a change, because
I'm tired, I'm tired of doing it all myself, so I
go home from school that day determined to
do it, determined to be the face underneath
the white sheet for once, and so that's what I
do,

I write my first poem. I lie down on the table and don't even bother throwing the sheet over my head.

and the next day I am the heart everyone
else is holding, with gloves on and hair back.
and there's a strange sense of comfort to it,
honestly. to lie down, and close my eyes, and
let someone else do the slicing and intruding,
to have the class point out what secret is
imbedded in every intercostal space, so that I
don't have to go looking for it all myself. to be
dug into instead of doing the digging. I'm so
tired of digging. so let me lie here, please. just
put on your gloves and get to it.

no matter how badly I want to get away
you never seem to loosen your grip on me.

I am caught up in you.
my limbs all tangled and knotted together.

and I've tried to get away.
I've tried getting distance,
I've tried getting time,
I've tried getting someone else
to replace you with,
but it never works.
at the end of the day,
you are still there.

I know you don't want me,
but I still feel you on my skin.

and I can never seem
to shake you off.

you are the one I talk about
late on friday nights
when darkness brings out
the secrets in all of us.

you are the one I circle
back to every week,
sitting on the couch
of my therapist's office.

you are the one written
between all of these lines.

it always traces back to you.

the soles of my feet
are calloused.
hardened and rough
from being worn down
and built back up again.

and I guess I could make them smooth,
I could sand off all the hardened skin
and leave them soft,
delicate,
vulnerable.
I could cut off the memory
of all the uneven terrain
I have crawled over.

but I leave it.
I leave it as a reminder

of the journey,
as proof of the pain I've endured.

I leave it because I am in awe
of how my body is always fighting
to protect itself,
no matter how many times
it is damaged.

I leave it because I am in awe
that even after all the times I've tried
to hurt my body,
it still knows how to rebuild.
it still knows how to heal.

well, you made it.
you survived.
the unbearable weight suddenly lifted.
the endless night broke into dawn.
the uphill battle led you to a peak,
and now you stand tall at the summit.

so
what now?
what do you do next?   ·
there is now air to breathe and room to grow
and time to fill and you did not plan for this,
you did not plan on having a life worth living.
and suddenly, there it is.

so,
what now?
how will you make the most of it?
how will you live the life
you never thought you'd get the chance to see?

*what could
have been*

a dream about you, part i:

we're half sitting, half lying down
on your floor, and the wood
is cool beneath my hands.

you lean over and kiss me,
sweet,
slow,
and then lean back down
on your elbow.

are you okay?
I ask, afraid to move.

your hand is on your chest,
fiddling with your necklace.
I feel . . . warm.

you say it shyly,
like it's something to be ashamed of,
and then tilt your head down,
sheepishly grinning at the floor.

me too,
I whisper back.

your eyes dart up to meet mine,
and for a second,
everything is calm.

we just sit there,
looking at each other,
holding desperately on to
the moment before I wake up
like it's all that we have.

little girl,
tall snow boots,
even taller banks of snow.
jumping from large footprint to large footprint
in order to make it through the sludge.

it's almost a game:
see if she can walk the path
without making a mark of her own.

one day,
not today,
she will decide to break away,
dragging her feet through
the cold and uncharted.

one day,
she will learn the importance
of leaving her own footsteps.

when you held my hand,
this messy world finally made sense.
but I'm sure it's just another memory
that you've filed away.
my thoughts are not that organized.
you are scattered all over the desk
and the floor and the walls
and I am too stubborn to clean them all up.

sometimes I close my eyes
and look at them as I try to fall asleep,
hoping that maybe you'll make your way
into my dreams.
and you do—
more often than I'd like to admit.

I'm learning that
it's the only place
where I mean as much to you
as you do to me.

you're stringing me along,
and I almost don't care.

I almost don't care
because it's so easy to get caught up in you.

when you rub your thumb over
the top of my hand,
I almost don't care
that this will hurt me in the end.

when your forehead
is pressed against mine,
I almost don't care
that we will crash and burn.

when you subconsciously show up
in everything I write,
I almost don't care
that you will be gone soon—

because I get to have you now.
and I am so in love with now
that I almost don't care
if it fucks me over later.

almost.

I cling to sheets like outstretched hands;
I clench and pull them tight.
instead of arms, I'm wrapped in blankets,
kissing the pillow goodnight.

I spend my days with darkness,
then I lead her to my bed—
since no one holds me close, I let
the night love me instead.

when I see you,
the violas swell.
the harp begins to play,
the woodwinds chime in,
and the entire symphony rises.

this is not a metaphor.

when I see you,
you're looking back at me.
you laugh as you miss your cue
and the music rushes past you.

this is not a metaphor.
don't turn this into a metaphor.

you look back at your music
and pick up your violin.

the cellos cut out.
the flutes fade away.
I live an entire concerto
in the five seconds it takes
for you to catch up to the world again.
and suddenly there is no more
you
or me.

there is only orchestra
and audience.

I don't want this to be a metaphor,
but it is.

you are the musician
and I am the crowd,
staying long after the show is over
hoping that maybe,
just maybe,
you'll come offstage
and become more than just a performance.
but you never do.

forgive me,
I don't know how to explain this
in any way other than metaphor.

when the applause dies down
and people put on their coats
and the theater goes back
to being hollow again,
I will still be here.
when the curtain closes
and you pack your things
and the chairs and music stands
are all put away,
I will still be here.
when the spotlight turns off
and the house lights turn on
and you are no longer a performer
but a person,
I will still be here.

you are not a performer,
you are a person.

I just hope to god you know that.

instead of wearing my heart on my sleeve,
I pasted it onto paper
and pressed print.

here.
take it.
it is not mine anymore.

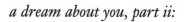

a dream about you, part ii:

we are holding hands,
fingers interlocked.
it's blurry
but I remember your mouth.
your laugh.
your voice.

you tell me you're sorry
it took you so long
to see me like this.

and I never stop forgiving you.

girl becomes young lady. young lady is loved by all her teachers. young lady hands in every assignment on time. young lady finds an empty stairwell at school and uses it to cry in during the day. young lady is bitter. young lady is hollow. young lady does not feel young or like a lady at all. young lady has a panic attack before writing an essay but still gets a good grade on it. young lady learns how to play ukulele and sings taylor swift covers on it. young lady buys a pencil sharpener and takes out the blade. young lady is timid. young lady is anxious. young lady likes to bake for all her friends. young lady is scared no one will ever love her. young lady is coerced into doing things she does not want to do by her boyfriend. young lady stays with him anyway because she thinks she deserves it. young lady doesn't talk to her family anymore. young lady is detached. young lady is tired.

you are not a gentle tune.

you are not a lullaby
no matter how many times
I fall asleep thinking of you.

you make me sick to my stomach,
but I spend all my time with you anyway.

I don't know how to digest our conversations.
you tell me about him
and I pretend I'm not nauseous.

you walk me home
and I dizzily fall to the bathroom floor.
when you ask if I am okay,
I laugh it off—
don't worry about me,
probably just food poisoning.

maybe you're allergic to something,
you reply.

and it takes everything in me
not to say *you,*
it's you.

I can't stomach even the thought of you.

we may not talk anymore,
but nostalgia lets us catch up.
I look at the picture
and you tell me how school is going.

I may not be near you,
but nostalgia brings us closer.
I look at the ticket stub,
and you sing to the music,
you hold my hand.

we may not be together,
but nostalgia gives us one last date.
I look at the program,
and you fall asleep on my shoulder
on the train ride home.

maybe it's naive to wrap my fingers
around the past so tightly,
but the future has not
offered me a hand yet.

at least nostalgia gives me
something to hold on to.

young lady becomes woman. woman shares
her secrets with the world. woman is scared
about it but does it anyway. woman does more
singing than she's ever done before. woman
forgets to weigh herself every day. woman is
growing. woman is healing. woman is not quite
there yet, but she's on her way. woman moves
out of her childhood home and finally feels
free. woman smiles at herself in the mirror.
woman cries in therapy. woman likes a picture
of herself for the first time in seven years.
woman cries in therapy again. woman is brave.
woman is kind. woman flushes her blades
down the toilet. woman eats breakfast most
days. woman is still on medication, but the
medication is working. woman hasn't harmed
herself in over four years. woman is strong.

woman is determined. woman is surprised she is still alive. but woman is grateful for it.

I am surprised I am still alive. but I am grateful for it.

you've got me writing cliché poems again

you make me want to
scribble out page after page
on how you are an ocean
and I am struggling to stay afloat.
how you pull me close
and push me away like the tide.

you make me want to
compare your eyes to the moon.
tell the world how much they shine
in the middle of the night.
write it out in ink,
and trace it over and over and
over again.

you make me want to
fill an entire book

with the tightness in my chest.
with the ache behind my ribs.
with the skip in my heartbeat
any time you're around.

you've got me writing
cliché poems again,
and suddenly I don't care.
because all of it is true.

I could write exhausted
metaphors about you
for the rest of my life.

a dream about you, part iii:

you're wearing an oversized t-shirt
dancing around the room,
and everything feels right.

I tell you it's getting late
and pull the comforter closer.
you run and jump
up onto the bed.

I turn to the side.
you drape your arm over me
and brush your lips on
the back of my neck.
and everything feels right.

I fall asleep next to you.
and everything feels right.

on love: the fine print

side effects may include headache / nausea /
increased sweating / changes in appetite / dry
mouth / delusions or hallucinations / insomnia
/ frequent outbursts of crying / agitation /
fatigue / an increased impulse to write sappy
poetry / dizziness / flushing of the face / an
increased impulse to write angry poetry /
changes in libido / blurry vision / an increased
impulse to write any sort of poetry at all /
heart palpitations / and anything else that may
cause you moderate to extreme distress / in
extremely rare cases, *love* has been found to
increase the risk of heart attack and suicidal
thoughts in younger patients / notify your
doctor immediately if you begin to feel you
are in danger of harming your heart / or the
heart of someone else / please be advised that

love does not actually rid the body of trauma
/ desire simply minimizes the perception of
it. / *love* is a controlled substance with a high
addiction potential / and it is not intended
for recreational use. / of course, you will use
it recreationally anyway / no matter the side
effects / because a little headache / nausea /
dry mouth / is a small price to pay / to cure
all your self-hatred (at least for the time being)
(and only for the time being)

there are days I feel
more art gallery than person,
more learning resource than human.

I am a walking museum exhibit
with every piece of my past
on display to the public.

how did we get here?
tangled up in a mess of
whispers and shaky hands.
sitting here, now,
with your thumb tracing the back of my neck,
and my nervous laughter turning
the television into background noise,
it's hard to pinpoint a when
or where or how or why.

I pull back for a moment,
trying to string the months together
into something that resembles you,
us,
and I can't seem to do it.
all I see are elbows and picked nails
and overrated movies.

but I remind myself, this is not the time.
here and now is pure simplicity,
the kind that comes only after
months and months of intricacy.
so, I decide I will not focus
on the complicated for now.

maybe I will not focus
on the complicated at all.

I'm not sure who to be anymore.

when depression found me
it dug holes into my body.
it shoveled me out like dirt
and filled in all the empty spaces.

now,
after learning how to stop
drowning from the inside out;
now,
after pulling out all the poison;
now,
after years and years of draining
I find myself free,
but empty.
there is more hollowed space

than person inside of me.

the depression may be gone,
but it took me along with it.

alternate universe in which I never found poetry
after heidi wong

1.
I sit on the grass,
pulling fistfuls of it into my small hands.
I hear someone start reading the first
few lines of a walt whitman poem,
but it does not interest me.
I do not lift my head to listen closer.

2.
my parents tell me they love me
and throw out the scale in my bathroom.
nine-year-old me never looks up fad diets
or buys a journal to count calories in.
the magazine pictures get pasted back
together.
the ink on every page slips back into the pen.

3.
a friend sits down next to me on the porch
that saturday night in late july.
I talk out loud instead of on paper
and the skin on my wrist mends itself.
there is nothing sharp for me to reach for.

4.
the image of the psychiatrist's office
fades from my memory.
the pills crawl back up my esophagus
and the bottles are resealed.
health class is the first place I learn
what the word *depression* means.

5.
my first relationship gets lost between
all the pixels on my computer screen.
the plane flies back to new york
and I remain unkissed.
I fall asleep on my friend's shoulder.

6.
the school stairwell at the end of the hall
does not mean anything to me.
my brain remembers the pieces of class
I missed while hiding in the bathroom.
my english teacher puts down the phone.
the school psychologist never gets my email.

7.
I look into her caramel eyes
and feel absolutely nothing.
I never have to wonder what this feeling is,
what it means for me,
what it means for my future.
I do not dream of playing
connect-the-dots with her freckles.
I spend the summer laughing,
carefree, unafraid.

8.
I get put into a different class
and never meet him.
the video games uninstall from my computer.
I watch the superbowl alone, and there are
no nightmares about his hands
or flashbacks for me to write about.
I go to sleep every night
in a bed he's never touched.

9.
my high school classmates open up my diary
and its pages are blank.
the whispers get pulled back into their lungs
and pushed out with other pieces of gossip.
there are no secrets to let slip
to the entire world anymore.

10.
I study biology in college
without a second thought.
life is clear-cut, neat, and simple.
for a brief moment in class, protein synthesis
looks a lot like creative writing to me.
but I shake my head and go
right back to taking notes.
this poem does not exist.
the pages are blank.
the book crumbles
and slips between your fingertips.
I am writing a lab report,
and you are reading your palms.

we never cross paths.
our lives go on.

bright are the hearts that long for a piece
that perfectly fits next to their own.
brave are the hearts that chase after love
when the consequences still are unknown.
strong are the hearts that continue to beat
when they're broken and falling apart.
so if you wish to be bright, or brave, or strong,
it's simple—just follow your heart.

forgiveness for what could have been
after doc luben

I used to be the best.
I used to fly through school with ease,
dreaming of all the perfect report cards
I would get in college,
in medical school.
then,
the depression found its way
inside of my bones.
my pencil would shake
from anxiety
as I took my exams.

I may be better,
but I am no longer the best.
and I'm trying to be okay with that.
I am trying to be okay with

not being the most intelligent
or the most successful.

but there is a voice in my mind
that tells me I could have been.

how do we forgive ourselves
for all the things we did not become?

for the decisions we regret,
the jumps we did not land,
the turns we missed that
could've led us to something beautiful?

I am still mourning the person
I was supposed to grow into.

I am still learning to forgive myself
for being the person I am today.

you are a surging thing—
you are all current and rapids
and I keep jumping back in
when you spit me out
worn down and breathless.

you are always spitting me out
worn down and breathless.

but the truth is,
I would jump back in no matter what.

why do I keep pretending
this will work?
why do I turn a blind eye
to all of your faults
and convince myself that
you are perfect?

I cut you open
and you are rotten to the core.
I beg to take a bite anyway.

this is what love is like,
I tell myself,
sour and overripe and beautiful.
I am lucky to get a taste at all.

you are not as sweet
as you are in my dreams,
but let me blame it on my taste buds
like I always do.

I want to believe you are perfect
for just a little while longer.

in the beginning,
god created the heaven
and the earth—
and the poets,
to bring the first two together.

we woke up in our own edens.
pulled out our ribs,
whittled them down into pens.
and when we finally came across
the tree of knowledge,
we did not eat from it timidly—
no.
we grabbed in handfuls.

the promise of suffering
only made our stomachs growl louder.

how could you want
to understand pain?
god asked.

how could you not want
to understand poetry?
we replied.

today, you called me out of the blue,
and when I picked up, all you had to say
was that you missed me.

I'm tired of all the metaphors.
I don't have any more
poetic ways to say this.

I just miss you, too.

I am always told
not to sacrifice myself
for my art—
but how can I not?

passion
derives from the
latin *pati*—
to suffer.

and maybe that is why
I pour my sadness
into art.
into faith.
into love.

maybe that is why
I spend so much time

turning the clay of my hurt
into sculptures of spirit.
into monuments of
the fire that refused
to burn out.

when I tell you
I am passionate,
I mean that
I am suffering.
I am hurting.
I am feeling so much
that it forces my jaw open
and begs me to speak.

when I tell you
I am passionate,
I mean that
years of self-hatred
created a backswing.

and now it is time
for me to follow through.

what became

when the world didn't end,
there was no party to throw.
there was no god to thank.
when the world didn't end,
a part of me still wished it had.
a part of me did not feel strong enough
to come back from it all.

I don't know.
I still don't feel strong enough.
but every day I wake up and I am still here.
so I have to keep on going.

and maybe it felt okay to die
when there was no other choice,
but there is a choice now.
and I choose to live.
every single day, all over again.

I choose to live.
I choose to live.
I choose to live.

apoptosis

there are parts of myself
I had to get rid of
to get here.

I used to think growing
was simply evolving,
but there is also shedding.
there is also loss.

there are people who hurt me
and shaped me
and found their way
into my cells.
in order to move on,
I had to scrub them away.

the sick cells had to be destroyed.
the damaged pieces of me had to be removed.

and sometimes I've found
that loss
can be a synonym
for growth.

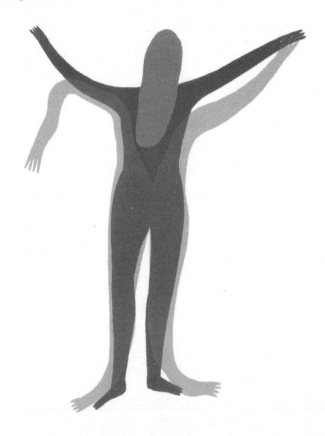

raspberries, metaphors, love, etc.

I let the raspberries you gave
me rot in the fridge,
and if I were a better person I wouldn't
turn this into a metaphor,
but it is one.
I watched all our sweet
turn to tart
turn to decay,
and now I have to get rid of you.

I let the raspberries you gave
me rot in the fridge,
but still, I do not throw them out.
I compost them.
because I am young and naive
and still have hope.
I still have hope that even after
all of this rotting,

we can continue to grow.
we can become something new.

and I know it wouldn't be pink-stained
and fresh and sweet and bursting.
I know it would be dark
and recycled and messy
and always kept outside of the house.
but at least it would be there.
at least it would be alive.

I don't hate you anymore.
I don't clench my fists
every time I hear your name
or grit my teeth at
the sight of your face.

I've spent too much time
waiting for a resolution
that is never coming.
and it is hard to forgive
without an apology.

now,
when I think of you,
all I do is hope.

hope that you

learned from me.
hope that you recognized
your mistakes.
hope that you never
do to them
what you did to me.
because then maybe
I can get past all of this.

it is hard to forgive
without an apology,
but I am trying to
do it anyway.
not because you
deserve the forgiveness,
but because I
deserve to move on.

I don't know how,
but I'm here.

I don't know how,
but I'm happy.

I don't know how,
but I will make this
a life worth living.

ten concord avenue

honestly most people think a therapist's office
is just a weird room with a long couch and a
big ticking clock and a shelf full of psychology
books and it's uncomfortable and you have to
sort out all your feelings and it's messy and
honestly that's exactly what my therapist's
office is like except the clock isn't really that
big and the psychology books don't bother me
because at least my therapist seems like she
probably read them and if she did then she
probably really knows her shit and if she does
then I don't have to feel as bad about paying
two hundred dollars an hour for someone to
tell me I need to learn to love myself which
obviously I already knew because I wouldn't
be here in the first place if I didn't absolutely
hate myself but honestly it's really not that bad

I mean the couch has a super-comfy pillow and there's a window out into some grass and trees so you can try to forget that you're in a fucking therapist's office but again I'm exaggerating it really isn't as bad as I was expecting it to be I mean it's nice to have a specific place to drop off tangled messes of thought and to only comb through them once a week when you're there and okay I'll admit that's not exactly how it works but I've never been good with brushing out knots on my own and now I'm just talking in metaphor like the stereotypical over-passionate poet I am and I don't know what I'm trying to say here but *just know it's not as scary as you imagine it to be.* everything seems stupid and pointless and like a complete waste of money until suddenly it's not because suddenly it's average and mediocre and only sort of a waste of money but hey I never said it would be a trip to six flags. I just said it wouldn't absolutely suck. it's still messy and uncomfortable and one of the hardest things I've ever had to do. just now I know it was also necessary.

do not assume
I am declawed
because I only scratch
when I need to.

do not assume
I am domesticated
because I hiss
before I pounce.

do not assume
I am soft
because I hide my fangs
under all this fur.

I am not the house cat—
I am the lioness.

and if you
try to cross me?

I will not hesitate
to bite you back.

your heart is a maze
I lost my way inside of.
say you'll take me home.

a dream about you, part iv:

you're sitting in my desk chair,
editing one of my poems.
you ask who it is about
and I try to force out a laugh.

there is a pause.
you lean forward in your chair,
closer to me,
and pick your words carefully.

what if the poem ends
with them getting together?

I don't know what to say,
so I don't say anything at all—
and then you kiss me.

and you kiss me.
and you kiss me.
and you kiss me.
and you kiss me.

let me be angry. let me be angry and hurt,
and upset and determined and tired
and ready and absolutely terrified.

let me be anxious and let me be frantic
and let me be furious, let me wear red.
let me bring it up in casual conversation.

let me act confident. let me cry about it
before I go to sleep and yell about it
when I wake up the next morning.

let me write about it. let me write about it
and write about it and then write about it
again. let me slip it under their doors.

let me publicize my trauma and let me hide
my face. let me avoid the dining hall and
skip over the comment sections but above all,

let me be angry. I read the articles, and
I am angry. I edit the poems, and I am angry.
at my core I am sadness and hopelessness

and regret and memories I don't want to relive
but all I can ever bring myself to be is angry.
so screw you. it's too late. I'm already angry.

if you are starving for kindness,
I will reach into my soul
and feed it to you,
spoonful by spoonful.

if you are desperate for sanity,
I will scrape the very last
pieces of it off my bones,
and hold it out in my hands.

the giving and the taking,
the offering and the collecting—
this is the only way
I know how to love.

cleveland, ohio, or the poem in which I try to not
hate myself as much

my brain cannot think of anything to say right
now, and that is okay. rome was not built in a
day. this poem was never going to be rome, of
course. it was going to be more like cleveland,
ohio. no one really cares about it or sees it
as something absolutely fantastic and you
wouldn't plan your honeymoon there, but it
can be a home. I'm sure there are people who
love it. wait. I have been told that comparing
myself to things that are mediocre still counts
as criticizing myself. let me try again.

rome was not built in a day. this poem was
built in a day but the sentiment behind it was
not. learning not to criticize myself is like
trying to unlearn an accent. no matter what

comes out, it's always there. it's just ingrained
into the way I speak. this is how I was raised
to talk. babies simply copy their parents. this is
what they sounded like. I'm getting off topic.
let me try again.

learning not to criticize myself is like trying
to unlearn an accent. it takes a while. I am still
trying to wrap my mouth around the vowels
of self-love properly. and I'm getting better.
I've learned to sound like the people around
me. but sometimes I slip back into it when
no one is paying attention. it's force of habit.
it's comfortable, it's worn-in. it's the beat-up
pair of combat boots I love too much to throw
away. wait. I'm romanticizing my pain. that's
not allowed either. let me try again.

I'm getting better. I'm holding myself
accountable, somewhere between slapping
myself on the wrist and gently nudging myself
in the right direction. but whatever it is, it is
working. and that's all I should be concerned
about. that's all that matters.

there. I did it. new combat boots. the crude
accent of confidence. a city built with
love instead of pain. and maybe it's not
as glamorous as rome. maybe it's not as
marketable. maybe it's not as awe-inspiring.

but I've heard cleveland is really beautiful this
time of year.

I used to have dreams about happiness.
always fuzzy,
always a little too far out of reach.
brief flashes of rose gardens
and park benches
and glowing birthday candles.

and I would always wonder,
is this the past
or the future?

is this longing
for a childhood I can
never get back?
or is this hope
for the person
I will become?

and I am so grateful
that it turned out
to be the latter.

I spent so many years
using delicacy like
a bandage.
holding myself together
with some apologies and
a dash of fear.

and I don't anymore.
I have grown into my skin
and stitched it shut.
I am strength,
perseverance,
audacity and grit
and spirit all sewn together.

but somehow,
you still undo me.

your voice pulls at the seams.
your skin cuts all the thread.

suddenly I am only
a mess of patchwork
and undone stitches.

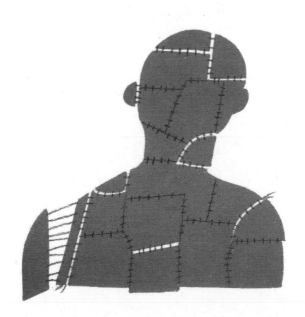

notebook pulled open,
lips pulled shut,
breath pulled in,
and heart pulled out.

—the words the words the words the words

usually loving you means
more forgetting than remembering.

loving you means
picking out the small moments.
you hand me a bag of trail mix
and I pick out all the chocolate pieces.
you hand me something that is not quite love
and I pick out all the purest parts.
when I hand it back to you,
it is only a jumble of peanuts and raisins
and the boy you kissed last night.
so I savor each bite of chocolate
and forget that my stomach needs more.

I mean, I know that my stomach needs more.
I know that I need more.
but still, I love you.
and loving you means forgetting.
it means forgetting you will never love me
because I want to keep loving you.

it means forgetting I don't like trail mix
because I want us to share the bag anyway.

the femur is the strongest bone
in the human body.
it's stronger than concrete,
more resilient than steel.
it's an homage to how much your body can
take.
how much you can persevere.

at two years old mine snapped in half.
my earliest memory
is of the car ride to the hospital.
and I want to say it was
the universe's way of telling me that
I'm too weak to survive.
that there's no point in fighting to live,
because this existence will give me
more than I can handle.

but none of that is true.
I did handle it, I did survive—
I wore a body cast for weeks
and relearned how to walk,
and my bone still shifted back into place.
my body knew how to repair
what had been broken.

I used to think of my injuries
as proof that I am weak.
now I just see them
as proof that I can recover.

I was taught to contain my emotions.
your mouth is full of lighter fluid,
they said.
do not turn people into matches.
so I held my tongue with a clenched fist
and let my throat catch on fire.

I have gotten so good
at finger-painting with charcoal,
and still,
it is hard for me to speak
without choking on the smoke.

so forgive me
for swallowing kindling
instead of telling you how I feel.

I would rather turn myself to ash
than risk you getting burned.

life had every intention
of burying me alive.
it showed up at my doorstep
in the middle of the night
with a shovel in hand
and asked how deep
I liked my graves.

it carved every poem
I wrote into stone.
turned my words into epitaphs
and asked me which headstone
I liked best.

how strange it must have been
to see me sit up in my casket
right before the burial.

how strange it must have been
to see me, not filled with anger or hate,

but love.

do not forgive me.
I am not sorry.

I do not owe you
an apology
for writing about
what happened.
I do not owe you
an apology
for how I choose to cope.
I do not owe you
an apology
for trying to make
the hurt not hurt anymore.

the hurt still hurts.

let me deal with this
in the only way
I know how.

honesty used to scare me,
but now, I wear it like
a perfectly tailored dress.
something that fits me,
something that moves with me,
something that feels more and more
comfortable with every added stitch
and cut of fabric.

honesty used to scare me,
but now, it feels just like
a second skin.
I can't imagine
walking around without it.

the seven deadly sins
lust

I do not know
what to call this.

I sing along to the radio
on the car ride home
and pretend she's there,
sitting in the passenger seat.

she is filled with fire
and I can feel her radiating.

she is filled with fire
and we are told to keep
our hands away from flames.

I do not know
what to call this,

because I've never felt the need
to reach for the spark.
I've always been able to keep my distance.
but suddenly,
the pull is too strong.
I do not care about anything else.

she is filled with fire
and I want to get burned anyway.

gluttony

I pour my feelings for her
into cake batter.
stir for thirty seconds,
slide it into the oven,
and let it rise.

when it comes out,
it smells like sugar and spice
and everything nice that
I want but cannot have.

so I stuff it down.
I swallow the memories whole
and hope the hydrochloric acid
is corrosive enough to break them down
into nothingness.

my stomach is starting to hurt.
but maybe that's just the
ache in my gut
from all this longing.

I've never been able to
tell the difference.

envy

you say he put his arm around you
and I feel my heart turn to stone.
I am nauseous
from all of this want.

you tell me what you like about him
and what doesn't feel quite right.
I try not to talk
and just nod my head.

you write a song about him,
and sing it to me as we sit on the floor.
I can't help but look for myself
in between the lyrics.

greed

look through my journals
and you will find her face
on every page.

I hoarded all the poems,
all the diary entries,
all the longing and pining
and wishing and wanting.

I told the world about
everything in my life—
but not her.
I wanted her
all to myself.
I wanted her
all to myself because
I knew what would happen
if the world found out.

can you blame me
for wanting to keep this
beautiful
and pure
and all my own
for just a little while longer?

sloth

if I leave my room,
I will see her.

she will smile at me
and I will compliment
her eyeliner and
she will laugh and
there will already be
a poem writing itself
behind my eyes.

but that poem makes it real.
it's proof of everything
that is right about her
and wrong about me.
a poem makes it real,
and I don't want it
to be real anymore.

so I do not leave my room.
I sit on my bed
and try not to
see her in every movie I watch.
hear her in every song I play.
find her in every note I sing.

I tell myself I will not leave
until these feelings go away.

they never do.

wrath

I am angry that
I have to feel this way.
I shake my fist at
a god I'm not even sure
I believe in because
maybe he is responsible.

I am bitter that
this world was not tailored
to fit me properly,
and I am bitter that
I am forced
to wear it anyway.

but mostly I am mad that
I was not able to keep it down
when it was swallowed,

that I couldn't be content
with half of my heart.
I am mad that now
I can't put the blinders back on,
because I finally know all of the
wonders they have been hiding.

pride

I do not change
the pronouns
when I write
about her.

I find the kaleidoscope
in my chest
and show it
to the world—
not with fear,

but with faith.

I do not write
to convince you
all these ripped seams
are beautiful.

I do it to convince myself
I can be stitched
back together again.

they tell me
to be careful
with my words.
to dull my pencil down
before I use it.

but I will not listen.

watch me split the earth
with my bare teeth.
watch the glass shatter
from my resonance.

and watch me
use my middle finger
to sign my name
under it all.

it's weird because I should be upset,
right?
my life is a complete mess—
barely getting by in school,
absolutely no plan for the future,
falling for the wrong people
over and over again.
I should be stressed.
I should be frantically trying to
put the pieces back together.
but I'm not.

my life is a complete mess,
and somehow,
I am the happiest I've ever been.

science suggests
that if time can move forward,
it can move backward as well.

if you break a bone,
you should be able to unbreak it.
if you bleed out,
you should be able to bleed back in.

scientists have figured out
how to unboil an egg.
how to cook it completely
and then uncook it.

how to go back in time
by moving forward.

I don't trust time
because I've traveled
through it before.

my heart was broken,
and then it was whole.
my thoughts were tangled,
and then I untangled them.
I lost happiness
and then found it again.

every day I go back in time
by choosing to move forward.

they all want to see me burn;
their hands are full of matches.
my fingertips are catching sparks—
but there will be no ashes.

even if you scorch my skin,
a fire will remain;
the sticks and stones you throw
are only kindling my flame.

I am not the right shape for any museum.
and I spent so much of my life
wishing I was someone worthy
of hanging in an art gallery.

but I am done trying to fit any frame.
I will lift the building's foundation
from bare earth
and let it follow the arch of my back.
it took me a while, but I get it now.
I do not need to shave myself down for them.

they will push out the walls.
they will lift up the ceiling.

this world tried to kill me,
but I do not hold a grudge
for attempted murder.
I came back with forgiveness,
with excitement,
tail wagging and eyes wide open
like a dog finding its way back home
after being left at the curb
over and over and over again.

I think that's the only way
to get through this life, really.

to pant and shake and lick your wounds
and *forgive forgive forgive*
once you find your way back home.

because if the world is to blame
for you losing your way,
then the world is to thank
for you finding it again.

every minute I have on this earth
is borrowed time.
I fought for it,
almost died for it,
and won it back.

I deserve to spend it
doing what I love.
I deserve to spend it
with the people I love.

and most of all,
I deserve to spend it
loving myself.

acknowledgments

to claudia gabel, camille kellogg, and the entire team at harper for continuing to believe in me and my writing, no matter how many middle-of-the-night emails got sent your way. I will never be able to express how grateful I am for the time, energy, and love you've poured into this book.

to andrea barzvi at empire literary for sticking by my side these past few years. I am in awe of how you're always thinking two steps ahead, and I would seriously be lost in all of this if I didn't have you to guide me.

to josh bell and the students in my poetry workshop for teaching me how to be proud of what I write. thank you for reassuring me that anything can be poetry—even my messy, sad, colloquial ramblings.

to the ones who just have a knack for making my world a better and brighter place. thank you for filling my life with inspiration and zeal. for offering me insight and fidelity. for the face masks, the movie nights, and the dining hall breakfasts. I appreciate you all so so so much. don't ever forget it.

and to you, always. whether you've been reading my work for five years or five minutes, thank you for giving my words a home. thank you for growing up by my side, taking the time to listen, and pushing me to keep going. it means more to me than you'll ever know.

Caroline Kaufman

—known as @poeticpoison on Instagram—
was only a freshman in high school when
she began posting her poetry online. Since
then she has amassed hundreds of thousands
of followers across social media reading
her work worldwide. Her debut poetry
collection, *Light Filters In*, was published
in 2018, and she was later named one of
Her Campus's 22 Under 22 Most Inspiring
College Women of the year for her work
destigmatizing mental illness through
poetry. Caroline grew up in Westchester,
New York, and is currently studying English
at Harvard University. When she's not
writing, she can be found eating pad thai,
harmonizing with the radio, and refusing to
believe she's growing up.